TREE-
HOUSE
comix
proudly
Presents

DOG MAN
MOTHERING HEIGHTS

WRITTEN AND ILLUSTRATED BY **DAV PILKEY**

AS GEORGE BEARD AND HAROLD HUTCHINS

WITH COLOR BY JOSE GARIBALDI

graphix

AN IMPRINT OF

Scholastic

Library of Congress Control Number 2020949707

978-1-338-68045-4 (POB)
978-1-338-68046-1 (Library)

10 9 8 7 6 5 4 3 2 1   21 22 23 24 25

Printed in China   62
First edition, April 2021

Edited by Ken Geist
Book design by Dav Pilkey and Phil Falco
Color by Jose Garibaldi
Color flatting by Aaron Polk and Corey Barba
Creative Director: Phil Falco
Publisher: David Saylor

CHAPTERS

MEET the CAST

DOG MAN: He has the head of a doG, the body of a man, and the heart of a HERO!!! He's lovable, brave, and enjoys chasing squirrels.

STRENGTH: Kindness   WEAKNESS: Easily Distracted

PETEY: Once known as the World's Most Evilest Cat, Petey is now working on becoming a better version of himself.

STRENGTH: Intelligence   WEAKNESS: Easily Annoyed

LI'L PETEY: Petey's son. He's a force for Goodness and Kindness, who lives with Petey during the week and Dog Man on weekends.

STRENGTH: Optimism   WEAKNESS: Can Be Annoying

MOLLY: An amphibious kid with a heart of gold and a propensity for silliness. She can fly and can move stuff with her brain.

STRENGTH: Psychokinesis   WEAKNESS: Stubbornness

SARAH HATOFF: An Investigative journalist/blogger who fights injustice wherever it lurks. She's an immigrant from Australia and has a pet poodle.

STRENGTHS: Bravery & Brains   WEAKNESS: Impatience

4

CHIEF: The fearless boss of the local police department. He's got the bravery of a warrior, and the heart of a kid.

STRENGTH: Loyalty   WEAKNESS: Impulsiveness

80-HD: A friendly sentient transforming robot who is a loyal friend to Li'l Petey. 80-HD sometimes gets destroyed, but he always comes back for more!

STRENGTH: Creativity   WEAKNESS: Malic Acid

ZUZU: Sarah Hatoff's feisty Poodle who bites first and asks questions later. Actually, she doesn't really ask questions. She's a dog.

STRENGTH: Tenacity   WEAKNESS: Holds Grudges

NURSE LADY (a.k.a. Genie S. Lady, RN, BSN): Her genius ideas and caring bedside manner are world renowned. Her quick thinking saved Dog Man's life.

STRENGTH: Moxie   WEAKNESS: Chutzpah

GRAMPA: Petey's dad. He's a selfish, egotistical meanie who currently resides in cat jail. Petey and Li'l Petey no longer associate with him.

STRENGTH: Intelligence   WEAKNESS: Arrogance

BIG JIM: Grampa's pure-hearted cellmate in cat jail. Sometimes he moonlights as a superhero named Commander Cupcake.

STRENGTH: Cupcakes   WEAKNESS: Cupcakes

Thank You,
Randy Kessler

"...love is something eternal.
It may change in aspect,
but not in essence."

-Vincent van Gogh

RiNG RiNG

RiNG

'SUP?

DOG MAN WAS INJURED?

IN THE Line of DUTY???

Chief's House

Some Random Dude's house

I'LL be right There!

QUACK   QUACK

HOLD ON, DOG MAN! I'm COMING!!!

WHITNEY WHITNEY WHITNEY

QUACK QUACK QUACK QUACK QUACK QUACK

HOSPITAL

QUACK QUACK QUACK QUACK QUACK QUACK QUACK QUACK

How is he??? Is he Gonna pull through?

QUACK QUACK QUACK

STEP 1.
First, place your Left hand inside the dotted Lines marked "Left hand here." Hold the book open FLAT!

STEP 2:
Grasp the right-hand page with your Thumb and index finger (inside the dotted Lines marked "Right Thumb Here").

STEP 3:
Now QUICKLY flip the right-hand page back and forth until the picture appears to be Animated.

(for extra fun, try adding your own sound-effects!)

REMEMBER,

While you are flipping,
be sure you can see
the image on page **21**
AND the image on page **23**.

If you flip quickly,
the two pictures will
start to look like **ONE**
ANIMATED cartoon.

Don't forget to
add your own
sound-effects!!!

Left
hand here.

Right
Thumb
here.

So let me get this straight:

Dog Man was drinking out of the toilet again...

... and the lid fell down...

...and hurt his fingers.

Bingo!

YOU SAID HE WAS INJURED in the Line OF DUTY!!!

No! I said "Line of **DOODIE**"!

You see, there was a really long **Line** at the bathroom...

...and we all had to go **doodie**...

...and, well...

You see, we... uh...

GET OUT OF HERE!!!!!

HOSP

YAAAAAAAA

Would you like to see him, Chief?

Yeah! Is he okay?

Yes! He's fine!!!

But he kept chewing on his bandages...

...and we couldn't get him to stop...

QUACK QUACK QUACK QUACK QUACK

...So we gave him a special collar!!!

Soon...

OH, NOOOOO!!!

DOG MAN! WHAT HAPPENED TO YOU?

He's okay, Chief!!! I Promise!!!

But why does he have to wear this silly Cone???

He only has to wear it for a few days!

But — but...

28

EVERYBODY'S GONNA MAKE FUN of him!!!

Well...

I'm glad he has a friend like you.

You'll protect him, won't you?

Sh-sure I will.

Good! See ya later!!!

B-b-b- bye!!!

QUACK QUACK QUACK QUACK QUACK

She noticed!!!

Oh, hi, Dog Man!

How come you're wearing that thingy on your head?

Whine whine whine...

You did?

whine whine whine...

are you okay?

Whiiine whine whine Whine whiiiine!

A FEW DAYS???

Hmmm...

Don't worry, Dog Man!!!

You stay here and enjoy a cup of pretend tea.

80-HD and I will solve this problem!

C'mon, 80-HD!!!

FLiP FLOP

Let's go to the Grand ballroom!!!

FLiP FLOP

FWA

FWA

SUPA PILLOW FORT

CHAPTER 3

Escape From Cat Jail

By George Beard and Harold Hutchins

Meanwhile...

Scribble Scribble Scribble

At Last! My Evil Plan is complete!

I just need **TWO** secret ingredients!

Hmmm...

41

Sorry, Grampa. I tried to warn you!

Only me and my new robot can use the Cupcake Exit!

THAT CARDBOARD HUNK OF JUNK CAN ESCAPE???

Well, it **COULD**— if I could make it work!

But I can't.

ON
OFF
EVIL   GOOD
♥

Maybe it just needs a battery!

OF COURSE!!! A BATTERY!!!

Meanwhile...

...while Dog Man was enjoying his pretend tea...

Lick
Lick
Lick

...Li'l Petey and 80-HD were upstairs in the Ballroom completing their new invention.

Okay, 80-HD. Let's test it out!!!

CLICK

49

We're all ready!!!

What?

? . . .

FLip FLoP FLiP

FLiP FLoP FLiP FLoP FLiP

Fwoop

An Umbrella?

Good thinking, 80-HD!

We did it, Dog Man!!!

FLIP FLOP FLIP FLOP

Now all we have to do...

KA-PLIK

...is get rid of this thingy...

whoosh

...and replace it...

KA-CLICK

...with the **Cone of Destiny!!!**

Now any time you get in trouble...

...Just press the button on top...

... And all of your wildest dreams will come true!!!

Are ya ready???

Who's gonna save the day???

Is it **YOU**? Are **YOU** Gonna save the day???

GO SAVE The DAY!

Oh, hi, Papa!

DOG MAN

FLIP FLOP FLIP FLOP FLIP FLOP

WHY is it THAT EVERY TimE I COME HERE...

...SomeThing DANGEROUS OR OBNOXIOUS HAPPENS?

That's how we roll, Papa!

Are you ready to Go home?

Already?

Yeah, and You're coming, too!!!

Yay! You can play with me at Papa's house!!!

He's not Gonna be **PLAYING!!**

He's not?

No! He destroyed **THREE** walls in our lab last week...

...**AND** he broke our DooR!

FLiP FLoP FLiP FLoP

So I'm putting him to **WORK!**

57

But, Papa—

AND NO "BUTS"!

You knuckleheads need to learn...

...That there are **CONSEQUENCES** to your actions!!!

FLIP FLOP FLIP FL

Aw, maaan!

I hate consequences!

FLIP FLOP FLIP FLOP FLIP FLOP FLIP FLOP FLOP FLIP FLOP F

crib crob crib crob crib crib crob crib crob crib crob

Meanwhile...

COPS

Well, well, well!!! Look who's back!

Hey, MAUDE! Check out Dog Man's head Gear!

HAW HAW HAW HAW HAW HAW!

He looks even more RiDiCULOUS than USUAL!!!

WHAT A DiSGRACE!

What an EMBARRASSMENT!

What A HUMILIATION!!!

You better hide behind that plant like you always do, ya **CONE HEAD!**

Yeah, **CONE HEAD!**

CONE HEAD!!! CONE HEAD!!!

click

KA-SHONK
BA-FLOMP
TRA-SKONK

BIBBIDY BOBBIDY
BOOYA

HEY!

Quit bugging me, Dog Man!!!

Can't you see I'm writing a very important letter?

CHAPTER 6

The PLAY-DATE

Okay, Robot...

...here's your battery!

Don't tell Grampa...

KLUNK

...but I borrowed it from his alarm clock!

HOW MANY TiMES have I TOLD YOU NOT TO TOUCH MY STUFF?!!?

ER—I mean...

...Beep-Boop. Greetings, Carbon-based feline!!!

It WORKS! It WORKS!

I Love you, Robot!!!

What do you want to do first? Hide-and-seek? Coloring Books? Go Fish?

No! Let's **ESCAPE!**

...er— I mean, Beep-Boop. Let's Go play **OUTSIDE...**

...and look for **Two** secret ingredients!

A TREASURE HUNT? Sweeeeet!!! What Shall we look for?

LiViNG SPRAY And Cannery Grow.

Why do we need **Them?**

Umm...

Meanwhile...

PETEY & Son

Fix those holes first...

cement cement

...then you can fix the door!!!

Let's Go, Kid. It's time to take your **BATH!!!**

But it's **DAYTIME!**

Too bad! You need to get cleaned up!

Because it makes them feel all warm and fuzzy!

Why?

BECAUSE iT TRIGGeRS DOPAMiNe ReSPONDeRS in The PeA-SizeD BRAiNS oF ALL The GuM-CHeWiNG SiMPLeTONS OuT THeRe Who've GoT NOTHiNG BeTTeR To Do THAN THRow THeiR LiVeS AWAY By SiTTiNG in FRONT oF A SCReeN ALL DAY!!!!

LAST week You both spent **ONE WHOLE DAY...**

...Making up songs about **DIARRHEA!**

Oh Yeah!

HA HA HA

That wasn't Strange. That was **HiLARiOUS!**

NOT WHEN YOU DO iT FOR NiNE HOURS!!!

HA HA HA HA HA

HA HA HA HA HA HA HA HA HA

Alright, Look: You can stay and play downstairs...

...but I don't want to hear a **PEEP** out of you kids!!!

Do you Hear me? NOT A Peep!!!

Okay, Papa!

Let's Go! Bye, Wally!

Peep!

Peep!

CHAPTER 7

A Buncha Stuff That Happened Next

By George Beard and Harold Hutchins

Meanwhile...

SHAKA SHAKA SHAKA

MAYOR'S **NEW** Rose Garden **KEEP OUT**
(especially Dog Man)

FWA

MAYOR'S New Rose Garden Keep OUT (especially Dog Man)

BWOOSH

HOSPITAL

HUFF HUFF HUFF

PLUP

DING-DONG

HOSPITAL

Oh, Look! A pile of slobbery roses!!!

I'll wash these off and give them to my patients!

That will cheer everyone up!!!

Meanwhile...

What do you mean, "No Longer Available"?

Well, Living Spray was banned due to complaints, right?

And they stopped making Cannery Grow...

...after the factory was destroyed in book #5, right?

THIS IS AN OUTRAGE!

As you may remember...

...Petey used to have a very bad reputation.

He was known across the continents...

...as the world's most evilest cat.

But all of that has changed.

Today, Petey is an upstanding citizen...

...And an ambassador for altruism!!!

Let's meet him now!!!

Heeeeere's Petey!!!

OPrah's Book Club

Well, hello, Sarah! What a surprise!

And how are you, little doggy?

Grrrrrr!!!

Be nice, Zuzu!

Yeah, be nice, Zuzu!

Petey, just a short time ago...

...You were widely known as a villain.

A ruthless bad guy.

An evil, scheming, Good-for-nothing scoundrel!!!

But you've changed.

Yeah.

Tell me why.

Well, I—

IF YOU'RE hAPPY
And You know it
Poop Your PANTS!

PBBT
PBBT!

IF YOU'RE hAPPY
And You know it
Poop YOUR PANTS!

I WEAR CLOThes SomeTimes!!!

No You don't.

Well look who's here! It's Li'l PeteY And MollY!

How are You two doinG todaY?

fine.

Are we on **TV**?

Yes!

TestinG, 1-2-3!

HeY, YA wanna hear a song about diarrhea?

NO SHE DOESN'T!

I told you kids to STAY DOWNSTAIRS!

But We're Hungry!

Yeah! Do you got any Potato chips?

How About something **HEALTHY** instead? I can cut up some carrots and broccoli?

You Know. The white stuff!

She means chip dip.

We don't have any chip dip.

Oh.

CHOMP

Munch Munch

Munch Munch

GULP

They taste way better with chip dip.

Well we're ALL OUT OF Chip Dip!!

That's okay, Wally!

You can get some for the next time I come over!!!

WOULD You GET OUT of Here?

Okay!

Bye, Wally!

Why does she keep calling you "WALLY"?

I HAVE NO IDEA!!!

CHAPTER #8
BECOMING
PETEY

We're back, **LIVE**, with Petey the cat...

...Who has agreed to give us a tour...

...of his **SECRET LABORATORY**...

...which is filled with all kinds of dangerous stuff!!!

It's an arsenal for Apparatuses of annihilation...

...and a depot for doodads of **DOOM!**

HEY, LOOK!!! THERE THEY ARE!!!

ER, I mean, Beep-Boop. I have detected the items we were searching FOR.

BOB'S TVs

We must ACQUIRE them at PETEY'S LAB!!!

...Your childhood was hard, wasn't it?

Yeah, but—

Your father didn't stick around, did he?

No, but—

And then you were orphaned.

Yeah, but—

But then something changed, didn't it?

ARE YOU GONNA LET ME TALK???

Certainly!

Okay, all of those things **DID** happen...

...but that's not **WHY** I became a bad guy.

Then why, Petey? Why did you turn to the dark side?

113

...Blew my under-

WHAT iS WRONG WiTH YOU TWO???

We're thirsty!

Yeah! Potato chips can get pretty dry if you don't have chip dip.

No offense.

ALRIGHT, ALRIGHT! WALK THiS WAY!!!

LAST Week You kids spilled cherry Juice ALL over the couch!

So **NO!!!** It's either sippy cups or **NOTHiNG!!**

Sippy cups.

Alright, then.

And don't leave them lying around on the floor!!!

We're back with Petey the cat.

But instead of **TELLING** us his story...

He's going to **SHOW US.**

For the record, I think this is a **BAD IDEA.**

Why?

We've got these **KIDS** with us. They're gonna **RUIN EVERYTHING!!!**

He's right! This **IS** A bad idea!!!

Aw, come on, Petey! Show us Your StorY!!!

Well, okay. I Got into trouble when I was Younger.

I made *some* bad choices.

And I got **CAUGHT!**

BY DoG Man?

No, it was **BEFORE** DoG Man.

Mean-while...

PETEY & Son

Hey, Robot! I don't think anybody is home!

Beep-Boop! Don't worry about it!!!

ROBOT!!!

GRAMPA? Was it You All Along?

OF Course it WAS ME ALL ALONG!!!

NOW Quit STANDING There Like A GUMDROP...

...And help me FIND WHAT I'm Looking FoR!!!

Right
Thumb
here.

NOW LOOK WHAT YOU MADE ME DO!!

Those TWO SiPPY CUPS Just CAME to LiFE...

...AND it's ALL YOUR FAULT!!!

Aw, don't worry, Grampa!

They're so cute and Little...

...What harm could they possibly Do?

PLINK PLUNK KLUNK

CATCH

SHAKA·SHAKA SHAKE!

SSSSSSSSS

135

"DON'T WORRY, GRAMPA...

142

143

What happened to 80-HD?

The mALic Acid in that apple juice...

...must have corroded his electro-gizzards!

He'll probably be okay, though!

147

149

Meanwhile...

Take me out to the BATH-ROOM...

...Take me out to Go Poo...

...My Doodie Smells Just Like Rot-ten eggs...

...And it's Starting to Run down my Legs!

Oh, if we don't get to the BATH-ROOM...

...And we CAN'T Find the dooR...

...THERE'LL be ONE! TWO!...

THREE PounDs of Poo on the BATH-RooM FLooR!!!

WHAT iS YOUR PROBLEM?

Actually, we DO have to go to the bathroom.

Yeah. SeriouslY!!!

And so...

SIX MINUTES LATER...

FLUSH! FLUSH!

You kids better quit goofing around! It's getting late!!!

Where are we going now, Petey?

To where it all began.

If You really want to Know whY I changed from bad to Good...

... it all starts here.

This is where my Mom and I lived after my Dad left.

HAPPY HOME SHELTER
WHERE KINDNESS RULES

We arrived with almost nothing...

...and things were pretty tough.

BUS STOP

And then one day...

...when I least expected it...

CLONING MACHINE
START
DNA

...her love became something new.

CLONING MACHINE
START
DNA

That's me, right, Papa?

Yep. That's You!!!

I didn't recognize it at first...

Sometimes, Love is so strong...

...it really **DOES** last forever and ever.

Are you saying that Love is **ETERNAL**...

...And even though its metaphysical characteristics may change, its invariable nature will remain pure, inspiring even the most hardened soul to transform into a benevolent altruist?

And it was working!

But the **Second** Sippy cup got an idea!

Carefully it Aimed its nose...

SPRAAASH!!!

Oh, boY! This is Gonna be---

HOSPITAL

SCREECH

OH, NO!!!

I'll help evacuate the hospital! YOU Fight those SiPPY CUPS!!!

SALUTE

Good Luck, DoG Man!

cLick

RAND·O·MON

O·MATO·PO

Right
Thumb
here.

While Dog Man duked it out with <u>one</u> sippy cup...

...the **OTHer** sippy cup was bent on Destruction!

CRASH

RUMBLE
RUMBLE
RUMBLE

It's Gonna destroy the Hospital...

... and there's no time to evacuate!!!

You Know what we must do?

INTRODUCING SMOOCH-O-RAMA

ALL NEW

The World's most Amorous Animation Technology

STEP 1: Turn to the next page and stare at the two Lovebirds.

STEP 2: SLOWLY bring Your face closer and closer to the picture.

STEP 3: Now RELAX Your eyes and watch the MAGIC!

How Romantic!

(PLEASE don't add Your own sound-effects.)

REMEMBER...

1. Stare at the image above with both eyes.
2. SLOWLY bring your face **CLOSE** to the page.
3. **RELAX** your eyes (try to look "past" the image).
BONUS: You can make them kiss again and again
by slowly moving your head closer to
and farther away from the image.

The struggle raged on...

... until things got really WHACK...

WHACK

...And DOG Man took the plunge.

SPLASH!

Sizzle
sizzle   Sizzle   Sizzle

THEN...

HeY! What happened to DoG Man's Robo-Suit???

PLUP

It's the Malic acid in this Apple juice!

It must have corroded his electro-Gizzards!

DARN You, APPLe Juice!

Who's Gonna Save us NOW?

Meanwhile...

I've Got to find a **WEAPON** or something!

But everything here is **BROKEN!**

Even this meerkat robot has lost her head!!!

But wait—

I can move her body with my mind!!!

Maybe all she needs is a **NEW BRAIN!**

SWOOOOP

MECHA MOLLY is GO!!!

So anyway...

Well, that was...

...Violent.

Thanks!

Welp, Good night, everybody!!!

Let's all play again tomorrow!!!

DoG Man, I have an important Job for You:

RoLL 80-HD home, okay?

And tomorrow, we'll fix him up as Good as new!!!

salute

salute

And so...

Hey, Look! There's Dog Man!

Would it be okay if he came with us on our date tomorrow?

Of Course!

Oh, boy, this is Gonna be **GREAT!!!**

You did, too!

I did Not!!!

And So...

I know, but Rudolph can fly, and Batman can't!!!

That's not the point!

Santa could beat up the

WOULD YOU KIDS PLEASE BE QUIET?

Just Five Minutes of Peace! That's ALL I ASK!!!

Just Five—

Hey!!!

What Happened?

Oh, Yeah. I forgot to tell You:

Your Lab broke.

CRUNCH
CRUNCH CRUNCH

Hey, WALLY? This might not be the best time to ask...

...but can I keep this Robo-suit?

WeLL, SURE, MoLLY! WHY NOT?

AS You can See, I've JUST LOST EVERYThiNG!

So PLEASE, HeLP YOURSELF!

...but it's been with me all along.

C'mon, Papa...

...let's go.

We can stay at DoG Man's house.

At least until we rebuild the Lab.

Okay.

I guess we don't have a choice.

We just lost everything.

Well, not **EVERYTHING.**

We still have love...

...and love lasts forever, right, Papa?

NOTES

by George and Harold

★ The musical interlude of Chief's dream (Chapter 1) is a parody of the song "The Greatest Love of All" by Michael Masser, with lyrics by Linda Creed.

★ Petey's red cardigan sweater and tie were based on the clothing often worn by beloved children's television host Mister Rogers.

★ On page 123, Petey is paraphrasing John 8:7 (NIV).

★ Petey's youthful "mistakes" and "bad choices" were chronicled in the graphic novel where he first appeared, *Super Diaper Baby 2: The Invasion of the Potty Snatchers.*

★ The title of Chapter 15 is the final line of the 1927 song "Stardust" by Hoagy Carmichael, with lyrics by Mitchell Parish.

★ This book was inspired by the two songs mentioned above, the quote on page 6, and the law of conservation of energy (a.k.a. the first law of thermodynamics).

HOW 2 DRAW

MECHA MOLLY

in **22** Ridiculously easy Steps!

215

CHIEF + NURSE LADY

in (17x2)+8 Ridiculously Easy Steps!

(x2) Now repeat steps 1~17 to make a SECOND PERSON beside the first. **BONUS POINTS** if you can make it look like they're holding hands. Awwww!!!

The WORLD'S MOST TeRRiFYiNGLY EViL SiPPY CUPS

in 26 (x2) RidicuLousLY eviL Steps!

To draw the other Sippy Cup, Repeat steps 1-9 on the previous page, then continue here ⟶

HOW 2 DRAW

in **23** Ridiculously easy steps!

ABOUT THE AUTHOR-ILLUSTRATOR

When Dav Pilkey was a kid, he was diagnosed with ADHD and dyslexia. Dav was so disruptive in class that his teachers made him sit out in the hallway every day. Luckily, Dav loved to draw and make up stories. He spent his time in the hallway creating his own original comic books — the very first adventures of Dog Man and Captain Underpants.

In college, Dav met a teacher who encouraged him to illustrate and write. He won a national competition in 1986 and the prize was the publication of his first book, WORLD WAR WON. He made many other books before being awarded the 1998 California Young Reader Medal for DOG BREATH, which was published in 1994, and in 1997 he won the Caldecott Honor for THE PAPERBOY.

THE ADVENTURES OF SUPER DIAPER BABY, published in 2002, was the first complete graphic novel spin-off from the Captain Underpants series and appeared at #6 on the USA Today bestseller list for all books, both adult and children's, and was also a New York Times bestseller. It was followed by THE ADVENTURES OF OOK AND GLUK: KUNG FU CAVEMEN FROM THE FUTURE and SUPER DIAPER BABY 2: THE INVASION OF THE POTTY SNATCHERS, both USA Today bestsellers. The unconventional style of these graphic novels is intended to encourage uninhibited creativity in kids.

His stories are semi-autobiographical and explore universal themes that celebrate friendship, tolerance, and the triumph of the good-hearted.

Dav loves to kayak in the Pacific Northwest with his wife.

TH DAV PILKEY!